There's No One Quite Like Grandpa

Written by: Wendy Spradley

Illustrated by: Lindsey Cunanan

Acknowledgments

This book is dedicated to my children Sydney, Shaely, and Bryce. Being a mom has been my greatest gift in life. Imagine my happiness and hearts content in now being a Nana! I'm overjoyed.

I'm forever grateful for all the love and support my children have had from each of their grandparents.

A special acknowledgment goes out to Darian McCollough for his assistance with the color design. Thank you for contributing to the beautiful illustrations by Lindsey Cunanan.

There's no one quite like Grandpa.
On him I can depend.

1

He's the one
I always
turn to.

He's a
special
kind of
friend.

2

We've shared
so much
between us

since the
day
I came
to be.

He would rock me
in my cradle.

He would
bounce me
on his knee.

When I turned into a toddler,
we had such a
ton of fun,

with

piggybacks

and

horsey rides

and picnics
in the sun.

When I got a little older,

we'd play golf or
maybe fish.

Then we'd stop to
get some ice cream,

or whatever was my wish.

When I chose
to take up
ballet
in a tutu
made of
lace,

he would sit through
my recitals with
a smile upon
his face.

He would
watch me
playing soccer,
cheering
loudly from
the side.

And when I got a
pony, he would come to see me ride.

I remember when we sold our house

and bought another home.
I left all my friends behind me-

and was scared I'd be alone.

But
Grandpa
said,
"Don't worry,"
when I went to
bed that night.
"You'll soon have
lots of friends, I'm sure."

And Grandpa got it right!

Now, middle school was kind of tough. I went a little nuts.

But Grandpa loved me just the same.

There were no 'ifs' or 'buts'.

He sat me down and
talked with me.

He let me have my say.

Then did
whatever he could do
to guide me
on my way.

I made the best of middle
school,

and high school years
were good.

Then I headed off to college,
seeing Grandpa when I could.

At my college graduation
where they gave me
my degree,

he was sitting front and center,
just as proud as he could be.

And then, of course,
I started work

and time was
not my own.

I could only talk
with Grandpa
if I called him
on the phone.

But though I didn't see him much
the way I used to do,
his love for me was just a strong,

and that I
always
knew.

On the day that I got married, there were tears in Grandpa's eyes.

He said he just had allergies but that was no disguise.

His baby girl
was all grown
up and so his
job was done.

His happiness was
such a thrill

for me
and
everyone.

24

As time went by he realized he needed extra care.

A safe and sound retirement home with nurses always there.

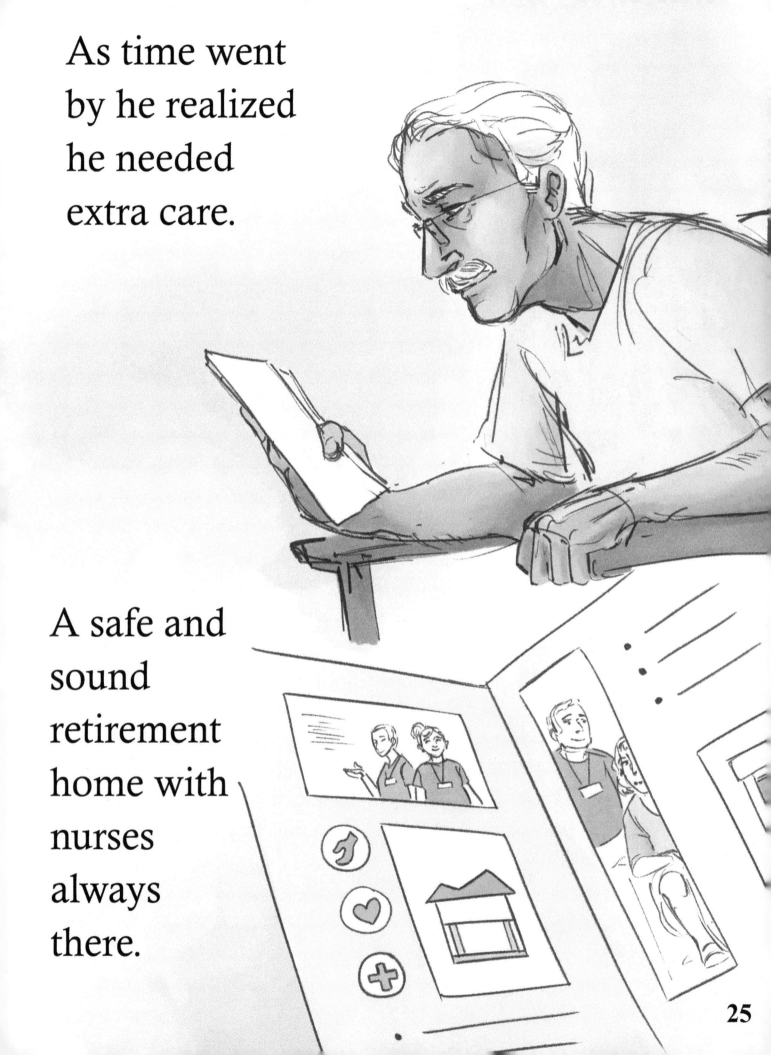

And so I helped him settle in

and tried to ease his mind.

"You'll soon have lots
of friends," I said.

"Just seek and you will find."

And I was right, as he had been,
so many years before

as Grandpa's made a lot of friends
who knock upon his door.

But still, he has one
special friend

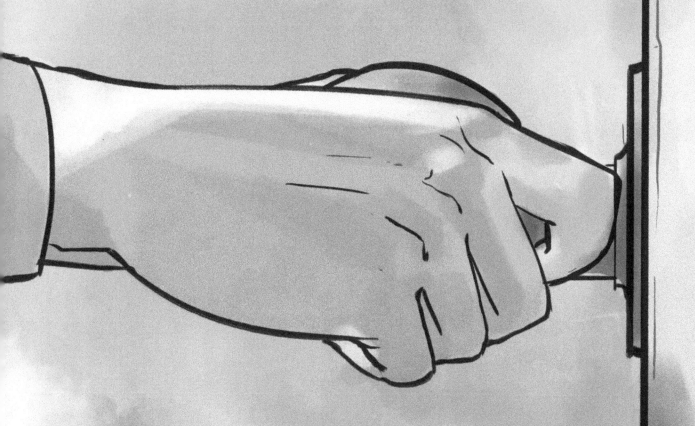

on that, we both
agree.

And can you guess?
I'm, sure you can.

That special friend
is me!